The Flood

Written by Rose Howell
Illustrated by Gary Undercuffler

CELEBRATION PRESS
Pearson Learning Group

Luke Scott went to bed feeling happy. Tomorrow was the first day of spring break. That meant there was no school.

Luke and his best friend, Trent, were planning to get together. They were going to practice batting and throwing baseballs.

When Luke woke the next morning, he heard a terrible sound. It was the sound of rain hitting the roof. He groaned as he looked out the window. He could barely see across the street through the curtain of pouring rain.

He found his mother in the kitchen. She had her right leg propped up on a chair with her crutches leaning against the table. She had broken her leg a week ago by tripping on the front step.

"Will the rain stop any time today?" Luke asked.

"I don't think so," she said, looking up from the newspaper. She sounded nervous. "It's been raining hard since last night. I'm worried about the river." Their house wasn't far from the Woods River. If there was too much rain, the river might rise.

Luke called Trent. They agreed to wait until the afternoon to see if the rain stopped. Then Luke went into the family room to see what his little sister, Maddy, was doing. He found her with her pet rabbit, Skippy. ✱

"How is Skippy?" Luke asked.

"He's a little scared of the noise the rain is making," Maddy said. It did look as if he was trying to find a place to hide.

Luke heard the telephone ringing. His mother had the cordless phone, so she answered it right away. Then, he heard her calling for him.

When he got to the kitchen, Luke was surprised. His mom was standing and leaning on her crutches.

"Hurry, Luke," she said, breathless. "Your father just called from work and said the river is flooding. Help me get upstairs."

"What?" Luke asked, confused. He looked out of the kitchen window. At the end of the street, he could see movement through the pouring rain. Suddenly, he realized it was a moving wall of muddy water!

Luke grabbed his mother and helped her hop to the stairs. He yelled for Maddy to follow them. Then he began to help his mother up the stairs, one slow step at a time. He looked toward the front door and saw that water was quickly gushing in under it.

When they got to the top, Luke then turned and started down the stairs. He had remembered he had left his prized baseball cards in the kitchen. Maybe he would be able to get them before the water rose too high.

Where was Maddy? He thought she had been behind them. He raced downstairs and splashed into the living room where water was rising fast. He saw Maddy trying to get Skippy.

"Maddy, come on! We have to get upstairs," he yelled, grabbing her arm and pulling her up the stairs.

Luke knew he had just one more chance to save something from downstairs. The water was already up to the first step.

He ran back down and waded into the living room. He found Skippy behind a chair and grabbed him by the back of the neck.

Luke struggled through the water toward the stairs. He thought he might have time to grab his box of baseball cards.

Then the front door splintered as a huge wave of flood water rushed in and knocked Luke down. He held Skippy tightly as his head went under the water.

Luke tried to get back on his feet, but he kept slipping. Finally, he was able to reach out and grab the stair railing. He pulled himself out of the muddy water and up the stairs. The water rose quickly behind him.

When Luke got to the second floor, Maddy ran to him. She took Skippy and hugged him.

"Mom, I don't think we're safe here," Luke gasped.

"Then we need to go up into the attic," his mother said, taking hold of Maddy's hand.

Luke pulled down the ladder to the third-floor attic. They all climbed up and sat by the window. Their street looked very different than it had that morning. Only the top half of the houses were visible.

"Mom," Luke sighed. "I think I lost my favorite baseball cards. They were on the kitchen counter."

Luke's mother reached over and hugged him. "I'm so sorry. I think a lot of things are ruined," she said. "We'll have to wait until the water goes down to see."

Luke turned to Maddy. She was drying off Skippy with an old towel she had found in the attic.

Hours passed. Luke looked out the attic window often. It looked like the flood water was moving more slowly. He was wondering if they would have to spend the night in the attic.

Then he heard a voice calling from outside. He saw a motorboat coming toward the house. “Mom, I think it’s Dad!” he shouted.

Looking out the attic window, the three were relieved to see Dad.

“I’ve come to rescue you!” Dad yelled. “Luke, help your mother and sister get down to the second floor.”

Luke helped his mother and Maddy down the ladder. Then, he helped them climb out the window and into the boat. Next, he handed Skippy to Maddy. Finally, he climbed into the boat.

Luke felt sad as the boat pulled away from their house.

“Dad, everything is ruined. I tried, but I couldn’t . . .” Luke sighed with tears in his eyes.

Dad placed his arm around Luke and pulled him close. “I’m so proud of you, son,” he said. “You did what was most important.”

Luke and his family stayed at his grandmother's house for a few days. At last, the floodwater retreated enough for Luke and his dad to return home. There were still a few inches of water in the living room and kitchen.

Luke waded into the kitchen. He saw a plastic box floating by the stove. He hurried over and picked up the box.

There inside were his baseball cards. They were a little wet, but okay. The plastic box his mom had given him had saved the cards. Luke smiled. "Not everything is ruined," he said.